D1368623

GIFT OF

John Warren Stewig

Carthage

[faint illegible library stamp]

Cur
PZ
7
L7725
Re
1992

Revenge of the small SMALL

Jean Little

Illustrated by Janet Wilson

VIKING

HEDBERG LIBRARY
CARTHAGE COLLEGE
KENOSHA, WISCONSIN

For my little sister Pat, who buried us in her village, and for our mother, who brought her the big box.

– J.L.

For my pal Laurie, whose help and encouragement have been invaluable.

– J.W.

VIKING
Published by the Penguin Group
Penguin Books Canada Ltd, 10 Alcorn Avenue, Toronto, Ontario, Canada M4V 3B2
Penguin Books Ltd, 27 Wrights Lane, London W8 5TZ, England
Viking Penguin, a division of Penguin Books USA Inc., 375 Hudson Street, New York, New York 10014, USA
Penguin Books Australia Ltd, Ringwood, Victoria, Australia
Penguin Books (NZ) Ltd, 182-190 Wairau Road, Auckland 10, New Zealand

Penguin Books Ltd, Registered Offices: Harmondsworth, Middlesex, England

First published 1992
10 9 8 7 6 5 4 3 2 1

Text copyright © Jean Little, 1992
Illustrations © Janet Wilson, 1992

All rights reserved. Without limiting the rights under copyright reserved above, no part of this publication may be reproduced, stored in or introduced into a retrieval system, or transmitted in any form or by any means (electronic, mechanical, photocopying, recording or otherwise), without the prior written permission of both the copyright owner and the above publisher of this book.

Printed and bound in Italy on acid free paper ♾

Canadian Cataloguing in Publication Data

Little, Jean, 1932-
  Revenge of the small Small

ISBN 0-670-84471-3

I. Wilson, Janet, 1952-   .II. Title.

PS8523.I77R4 1992   jC813'.54   C92-093941-4   PZ7.L57Re 1992

British Library Cataloguing in Publication Data Available
American Library of Congress Cataloguing in Publication Data Available

Patsy was the baby of the family.

"The crybaby," teased her big brother Jim.

"The kindergarten baby," laughed her big sister Jane.

"The lowly infant," said her brother Hugo, who was just one year older.

Patsy put her hands over her ears.

"I am not, am not, am NOT a baby," she yelled. "Daddy, I'm not an infant either, am I?"

Dad grinned down at her.

"No," he said. "You're just the small Small."

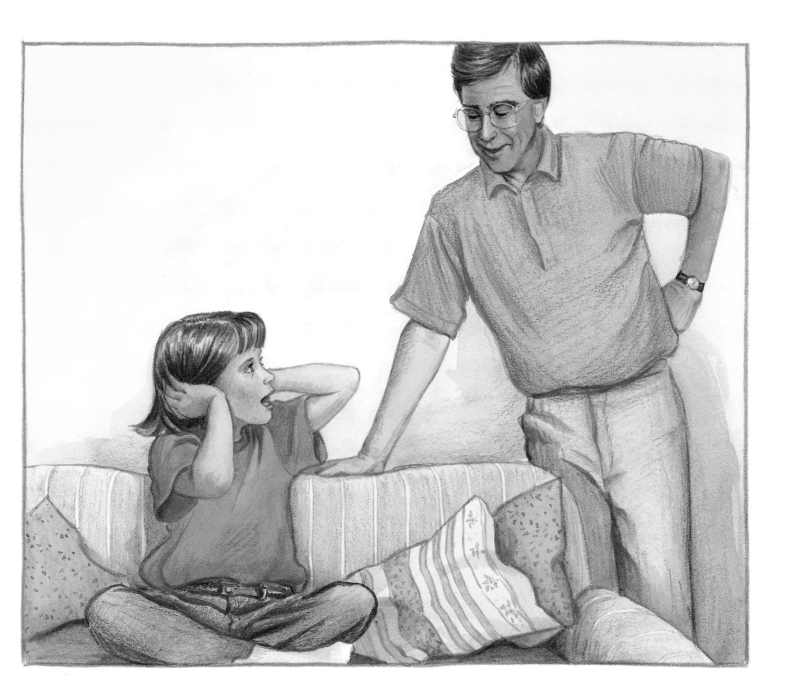

Patsy hated being teased. But she hated being left out even more.

"I can so keep up," she told the others. "I'm not too little. I won't be in the way. I can help!"

When the older children got chicken pox, she proved it. She brought Jim glasses of ginger ale – with ice cubes. She loaned Jane her very own copy of *Ramona the Pest*.

And she gave Hugo a toy for his hamster.

"For such a lowly infant," Hugo said, "you're not half bad."

Then Jim and Jane and Hugo got better and Patsy got sick.

"You have to stay in bed till your fever goes down," Mum said.

"Jane, read me a story," Patsy begged.

Jane was too busy.

"Jim, will you lend me your Lego?"

"No way," said Jim. "You'd lose half the pieces."

"Hugo, may I have your hamster in bed with me? I'll be very gentle with him," Patsy promised.

Hugo was busy too. "He's asleep," he said.

On Monday morning, Patsy got up, but she still had too many spots to go back to school. She was lonely and bored and itchy.

"I'm sick of TV and books," she whined. "I want something to DO."

That night, Dad brought home a big box.

"What's that?" the other children demanded, crowding around.

"It's a surprise for the small Small," said their father.

Patsy sat on the floor and opened the box while the others watched. Inside was a giant package of construction paper, all different colours. There was an envelope of bright origami paper too. There were crayons and markers and chalk. There were paper clips, toothpicks, pipe cleaners and string. There was a fat glue stick and a box of plasticine. There were gold and silver gummed stars and sequins. There was even a small pair of scissors.

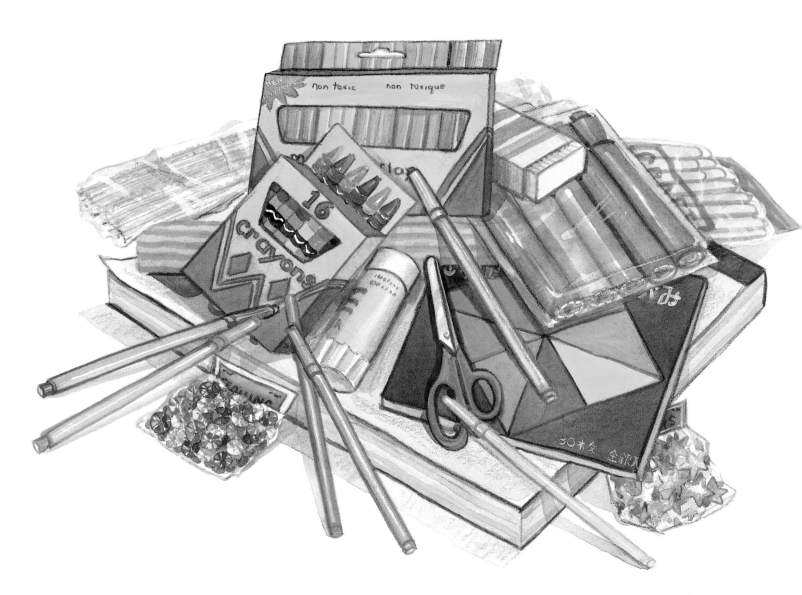

Patsy took all the things out, one by one. Then she put them all back.

"What are they for?" she asked her father.

"They're for you to use however you like," Dad said.

Patsy looked sideways at the others.

"Do I have to share?" she asked.

"You do not," said her father.

"What are you going to make, Patsy?" Jane asked, staring at the box.

"I don't know yet," Patsy said softly.

"You could make a space station," Jim started to say.

"You could make a neat dinosaur," Hugo began to explain.

"You could make a toy theatre," Jane butted in.

Their little sister jumped to her feet. She did not say a word.
She just grabbed the big box and tugged it into the dining room.
Then she slammed the door.

The next afternoon, when the older children came home from school, they found Patsy making a village. She had already finished three paper houses, one street sign and a dog.

Jim picked up the dog. "What's this?" he asked.

"It's a dog," said Patsy proudly.

Jim thought of the great space station he could have made.

"It looks like a sick cow to me," he said.

Jane remembered the beautiful toy theatre she had wanted to help Patsy make. She reached for the street sign.

"Look how she's spelled MAPLE," she giggled.

Hugo looked. He did not see what was wrong with Patsy's spelling but he did not say so. He gave a loud laugh instead.

The next day, Patsy's village was much bigger. There was a whole street of houses, a school and a church.

"That steeple looks like a bent witch's hat," Hugo said. "I'll make you a better one."

He reached for the package of construction paper. Patsy shoved his fingers away.

The next day, Patsy's village had a firehall, a library and a park. The park had a swing in it. If you touched the swing with the tip of your finger, it moved gently back and forth.

"Wow!" said Jane.

Patsy had just finished making a town sign. When she set it up, the others burst out laughing.

THE SMALL TOWN, it said.

"Not bad," Jim told Jane and Hugo. "Pretty sharp, in fact."

Patsy pretended not to hear, but her cheeks got very pink.

Even on the weekend, she still would not let them help. Every time they looked at her village, Jim and Jane and Hugo gazed longingly at the markers, the stars, the plasticine and the fat glue stick.

On Monday, when the older children were in school again, Patsy made a horse. She loved it.

"What's THAT supposed to be?" they asked.

Patsy knew they were going to be mean. She shook her head and shut her lips tight. She would not look at them.

Jane studied the horse.

"I don't think it's so bad," she said, "...for a four-legged duck."

When they ran off, laughing, Patsy picked up her horse and held it against her cheek.

"I think you are beautiful," she whispered to it.

On Tuesday, the three older children were late coming home because of piano and swimming lessons.

"Where's the infant?" Hugo asked as they sat down to eat.

"Asleep, I hope," Mum said. "She felt a bit feverish so I put her to bed early."

"Let's inspect the village," Jane said to the boys.

"There's a pond now," Jane cried, "with water in it! Look."

"She's made smoke coming out of this chimney," Hugo said. "Neat."

But Jim was staring at the square of green grass next to the church.

"Hey," he said, "she's made a cemetery— and buried people in it!"

Jim stared at the first tombstone.

Jane's eyes went wide as she read
the stone next to Jim's.

Hugo read the third one.
He gasped.

When the three children came away from their little sister's village, they were very quiet. Mum looked at their faces.

"You seem tired," she said. "Maybe it's time everyone went to bed."

Nobody argued. They went to their rooms without talking to each other.

At breakfast, Jim said, "I put some of my Lego in by your village, Patsy. I thought you might like to use it for something."

"I would love to," she breathed.

"I put my hamster there too," Hugo said. "I thought you might like him to be an animal in your zoo."

"He'd be perfect!" Patsy cried. Her eyes were shining. "He could be the woolly mammoth."

"I thought up a wonderful story to tell you the minute I get home," Jane put in. "It's got a princess and a dragon both. I know how you love princesses and dragons."

Patsy beamed at her.

"Thank you, Jane," she said.

When they had gone to school, Patsy climbed onto her father's lap. She hid her face in his shoulder.

"I buried Jim and Jane and Hugo in the graveyard in my town," she confessed.

"I saw," Dad said.

"It was mean," Patsy said in a small voice. "I wrote bad things."

"It did them a world of good," her father said, hugging her.

Patsy went in and looked at her small town. She saw Jim's box of Lego. She watched Hugo's hamster. Then she stared at the cemetery for a long time. At last, she sat down and went to work.

And when her brothers and sister looked at their graves that night, they found a tiny bunch of paper flowers on each one.

The small Small had changed the words a little too.